I0784354

fractured

To receive new fiction, contest deadlines,
and other curated content right to
your inbox, send an email to
newsletter@fracturedlit.com

© 2024 *Fractured Lit*. Published annually by *Fractured Lit*. All rights reserved. No part of this publication may be reproduced or reprinted without prior written permission of *Fractured Lit*. To contact an author regarding rights and reprint permissions please contact *Fractured Lit*. www.fracturedlit.com

Fractured Lit Volume 4
Stories Selected by Morgan Talty
Edited by Tommy Dean

Front cover by Cynthia Young and Emelie Mano
Interior design by Cynthia Young and Julianne Johnson

ISBN: 979-8-9901838-1-0

fractured

volume 4

contents

introduction

What does it mean to live?

Over the past three years, I have been ruthlessly blessed: I've published two books and (shhh!) sold a third; I landed a full-time position at the University of Maine, Orono, after adjuncting everywhere and anywhere in Maine to make money, driving in a '99 green Hyundai whose underbelly was held together with welded-on lawn mower parts and clothes hangers to pass inspection, and on February 27, 2023, my wife and I welcomed Charlie, our son, into the world.

The number of "highs" I've experienced are many, but the number of "lows" I've experienced might equal the "highs"—at least that's how it feels: My father is long gone; my mother died in 2021, several weeks after she said to me—in her sweet, child-like voice she used to talk to me when she really, really wanted something—"When are you going to give me a grandbaby?"; and my sister, ten years older than me and an addict her whole life, was coming back from a detox center and the car crashed, which caused the vertebrae in her neck and back to shatter and throw splinters of bone down her arms. The splinters were removed during surgery but now she is mostly metal and suffers severe nerve pain. Oh, and for a month, my wife and I had to wait to find out whether our son Charlie had cancer. He does not. I like to think his grandparents had something to do with it, wherever they are in that place we know nothing about but will know all about when our time comes, at which point we will all look back and say: "This came faster than expected."

Literature has always taught me and reminded me that the lows do not equal the highs. That is the truth: great writing deals with matters of the heart in ways knowable as the back of our hand and as unknowable as what awaits us on "the other side."

As I read for *Fractured Lit*'s annual anthology and compiled these stories, I encountered great literature with the kind of heart that reminded me how to find equilibrium. The stories in this collection—each one raw, unfiltered, and deeply human—offered solace, insight, and a profound sense of connection.

"Protocol for What to Do after Hearing Another Rape Story in Exam Room Five" presents the emotional and procedural complexities faced by healthcare professionals dealing with sexual assault survivors. The story blends procedural advice with surreal elements, underscoring the psychological toll on the caregiver, a reminder that life's cruelties are sometimes faced in the most sterile environments, yet the wounds cut deep.

"Departures" captures a mother's struggle with her daughter's departure, intertwined with memories of her own defiance. The cyclical nature of the narrative and the evocative imagery of planes and flowers meditate on separation and resilience, echoing the emotional farewells and hopeful returns that life is full of.

"The Eulogy Competition" examines sibling rivalry and family complexities through a competition to write a eulogy. The layered approach to memory and loss adds depth to the characters, resonating with the bittersweet truths of familial bonds.

"Could Die for Just a Wee Lie-Down" weaves together the exhaustion of motherhood with a haunting memory of a beached whale. The evocative language and imagery create a powerful meditation on weariness, responsibility, and the quiet moments of life's relentless demands.

"Act As If" delves into the mundane yet profound details of a woman's life as she navigates recovery and self-rediscovery. The narrative's focus on everyday objects and moments provides a rich, textured portrait of resilience and the quiet triumphs of survival.

"Newfoundland" follows a protagonist's journey through loss and self-discovery across various cities and landscapes. The narrative mirrors the internal quest for meaning and healing, leaving the reader with a sense of the vast, untamed terrain within each of us.

"The Last Laugh" is a darkly humorous tale about a mother and daughter's visit to a funeral home. The sharp wit and poignant moments offer a memorable commentary on grief and societal expectations, reminding us that humor is often a companion to sorrow.

"True Story" blends reality and imagination, exploring themes of truth, perception, and memory. Its layered approach invites readers to question the nature of storytelling itself, a reminder that our lives are narratives we both write and are written into.

"This Time of Death" reflects on life, death, and the passage of time through the aftermath of a neighbor's death. The contemplative narrative resonates with the quiet reflections we all have in the face of life's inevitable end.

"Diorama of Star-Crossed Lovers Driving at Night" vividly depicts a couple's perilous night journey, capturing the tension and beauty of their relationship. The rich descriptions and emotional depth underscore the fragility and passion that love entails.

"Those Who Seek" explores the search for meaning and connection amidst chaos, set in a crowded stadium with anticipation of a mysterious event. The narrative's backdrop becomes a compelling stage for introspection, reflecting our collective longing for purpose.

"Safe Passage" tells of a son's attempt to fulfill his father's final wishes. The exploration of memory, legacy, and the sea as a metaphor for life's journey is deeply moving, offering solace in the face of life's greatest unknowns.

"Hug Me" explores themes of maternal love, loss, and coping with separation through the innovative metaphor of a duplicating app. The story's emotional depth highlights the ways technology can mirror and magnify our deepest desires and fears.

"Thirteen" captures the innocence and transformative experiences of adolescence during a teenage sleepover. The blend of magic and reality enhances its charm and depth, a reflection of the wonder and fear that define growing up.

"The Children" offers a unique blend of horror and social commentary through the macabre return of deceased children and the community's response. The unsettling atmosphere and portrayal of parental grief make it an unforgettable exploration of the boundaries between life and death.

"When the Giant Breathed" transports the reader to a fantastical world where a Sleeping Giant awakens, impacting the villagers with fear and wonder. It reminds us of the unknown forces—within and outside us—that shape our lives in ways we can never fully comprehend.

"Self-Preservation" offers a poignant look at mental illness through the depiction of Barbara's compulsive hoarding. The story's detailed descriptions and character development linger in the mind, a testament to the burdens that we carry in silence.

"We Went to the Museum" handles family dynamics and the impending loss of a loved one with sensitivity and realism. The museum setting serves as a poignant backdrop, where the echoes of the past meet the uncertainties of the future.

"Flesh Wounds" draws the reader into a life-or-death situation with visceral immediacy. The protagonist's reflections reveal layers of complexity and human vulnerability, resonating with the fragile balance between life and loss.

"The Life of the Mother" delves into themes of grief, motherhood, and the stark realities of medical crises. Its emotional intensity and exploration of difficult choices confront the reader with the weight of love and the inevitability of loss.

So again, I ask: what does it mean to live? There are countless answers, I think. But from these stories, I'm left with this answer: To live is all the answers and more. It's to taste the things we love and hate. It's to be disappointed. Happy. Sad. Broken. But to live—to truly live—is to be reminded of how precious this life is.

Remember what we all will say right before our end: "This came faster than expected."

In the midst of all the lows—grief never goes away—I found solace in these stories, in the words of these twenty writers who, knowingly or not, offered me a lifeline through their art. This collection of twenty stories, each unique yet profoundly interconnected, played a pivotal role in a healing I didn't know I needed. These stories didn't just distract me from my pain—they confronted it, mirrored it back to me, and ultimately transformed it into something bearable, even beautiful. They became my companions in the dark, illuminating the path forward when everything else seemed obscured. Each story, in its own way, spoke to the raw, unfiltered emotions that I was grappling with, and in doing so, they helped me make sense of my own narrative.

So please hurry and read these stories before you say to yourself the words right before you learn the truth.

—Morgan Talty

1

Protocol for What to Do after Hearing Another Rape Story in Exam Room Five

MARGARET ADAMS

1.   Make sure your patient is safe. Hope that you gave the appropriate caveats when you told them that this visit is confidential, and make sure they don't have any plans to hurt themselves or others. If they're a minor, you may have

to call Child Protective Services. If you didn't properly warn them that this could happen if they disclosed this kind of harm, well, you are a huge asshole. Too late now. Let's just hope you did.

2.   Once you've made sure they're safe in an immediate, physical, legal kind of way, start saying the right things. Tell them it's not their fault. Tell them they're not alone. Don't tell them, *Hell, yours isn't even the first rape story I've heard TODAY.* When you get the urge to say this, lean in hard to the open-ended questions. *What do you need?* Offer forensics, advocacy, Plan B, antibiotics, therapy, water, tissues. Respect whatever they want. Don't offer your own thoughts or opinions.

3.   After they've left, document. In your note, don't use the word *alleges.* Don't put "sexually assaulted" in quotes like you're not sure. You would not write "patient alleges broken arm," so don't let the reflexive doubt of women seep in here. Don't say simply that they were upset; describe instead the way their face didn't move when they cried.

4.   At this point, even though you're done, their story is alive in your skin. Your brain is a lurching mammal, the large kind, but the large kind that eats grass and dies easily. Notice this.

5.   Look down and realize that your shoes feel funny and that is because you now have hooves.

6.   Tell your coworkers you are leaving for the day. See if they notice if you look different. They don't, or you don't, it's unclear.

7.   Go outside and lie on the grass. Don't eat any of it, yet. Feel your limbs press into the ground. Try to loosen, let the earth do the work of holding your bones up. Your face feels furry. It's hard to tell because your eyes are widely set now.

8.   Get up and run around. Run around and around and around. Avoid the road, but also poorly lit areas. It's hard to do both, but try. The sun will set soon.

9.   If you are hit by a car, lie stunned on the side of the road, and know that the worst part is that if you live, you're going to have to get up and keep going, eat more grass and have fawns and rub your rough fur on the sides of trees and probably, statistically speaking, get hit by another car, because deer are basically the pigeons of suburban America, and modern cars are pretty durable. Because that's how society has dealt: we've made stronger cars.

10.   Run home. Your hooves clop on the walkway to your door. Swivel your eyes and hold your keys like a weapon until you put them in the lock.

11.   Sleep. Don't remember how you got into bed. Don't remember if you did or didn't watch a few hours of television. Don't remember if you drank water, or how.

12.   Wake up. Pull pants on over your human legs. Pat moisturizer on your cheeks. Go to work. Ask the questions. Say the right things. Follow the protocol.

✑

MARGARET ADAMS's stories and essays have appeared in over two dozen publications, including *The Threepenny Review, Best Small Fictions 2019, Joyland,* and *Pinch*. She is the winner of the Blue Mesa Review 2018 Nonfiction Contest, the Pacifica Literary Review 2017 Fiction Contest, and a Notable in *Best American Essays 2019*. She is a healthcare worker as well as a writer, and she currently lives in Vermont.

2

Departures

SANDRA ARNOLD

A plane ploughs through the clouds as she scrubs and cleans the plugholes in the washbasins and the kitchen sink and the laundry and another plane ploughs when she mops the floors and washes the benches and polishes the windows and another plane ploughs when she reorders all the cupboards and drawers until finally everything is done and she can go into her garden where the only sounds she hears are birds singing in the trees that her daughter used to climb and she cuts camelias from the bush her daughter used to love because the blooms were pink and then she goes back into the house to sit in the glint and the gleam and breathe in the scent of flowers as she recalls her father's fury in the days before Facebook and Zoom and email when she told him she was leaving for the other side of the world and he roared that her mother had never stopped crying since and insisted she wait until they were dead before she left but she didn't wait and she said it was her right to choose her own life so this morning at the airport before her daughter departed she told her to be happy and they both knew there was Facebook and Zoom and email and after she waved goodbye she headed home and scrubbed and cleaned and polished for the rest of the day with the roar of planes inside her head and now the sun sinks and the sky glows pink and she drops into a chair in the pink-tinged dusk with her eyes closed and a pink camelia held to her cheek.

SANDRA ARNOLD's work includes her two 2023 published books, *The Bones of the Story* (Impspired Books, UK) and *Where the Wind Blows* (Truth Serum Press, AU), and her 2019 books, *The Ash, the Well and the Bluebell* (Mākaro Press, NZ) and *Soul Etchings* (Retreat West Books, UK). Her short fiction has been published internationally and received nominations for Best Small Fictions, Best Microfiction, and the Pushcart Prize. She has a PhD in creative writing from Central Queensland University, Australia. Learn more at www.sandraarnold.co.nz.

3

The Eulogy Competition

LISA FERRANTI

My father tells all three of us to write a eulogy and he'll decide who gets to deliver theirs at our mother's funeral in five days. Tom's jaw sets, determined. Diane nods, eager to please. I narrow my eyes at Dad, resenting the competition he fuels between us, even as adults. I'm the youngest, nicknamed Flaky Suzy, and I will not win. The sweaty-palmed funeral director ushers us to the door. The flowers in the hallway are plastic but I swear I can smell gardenias, Mom's favorite.

We have our marching orders and go our separate ways. Being the least responsible, I've been assigned relatively few duties, so I head to the coffee shop with my notebook and consider what to say about Mom.

Should I tell about the time she won top prize for flower arranging at the state fair? How I'd never seen her smile so wide, not even when Tommy was state swimming champ.

Or about when she was PTA president and planned the best school carnival ever, with a dunking booth. For one dollar we could try to dunk the principal and teachers. But that's more Tom's story, since he holds the record from that day.

The story about finding our dog, Lucille, is a good one. Dad was at work and the four of us searched for hours. Tom and Diane pedaled off on their bikes, and I rode in the car with Mom. She drove slowly and I hollered *Lucy* out the window. Diane is the hero of that tale, though, finding Lucy trapped inside our neighbor's pool fence and bringing her home just as we pulled into the driveway.

Should I tell about the times Mom let me play hooky from high school? How she would call the office to say I had a cold and would be absent, my face growing hot, not with fever but with excitement that I'd get to spend the day alone with her. How we'd play gin rummy for hours. She smoked while we played, catching ashes in an old coffee can, sometimes letting me smoke too. At the end of the day, we opened windows, sprayed air freshener. Before I'd go to change out of my fake sick-day pajamas, she'd hand me the coffee can, lid on, to hide in my bedroom closet, a place Dad would never venture.

Should I tell about the time she confided to me she wanted a tattoo but couldn't decide what to get? I'd sketched a rose as a suggestion. "Maybe my initials instead," she said, and I penned a scripty *MS*. She smirked, saying we'd have to add her middle initial or it would look like it stood for *multiple sclerosis*. She never got a tattoo, but I wonder if we breathed life into the idea? If that was the day her body birthed the germ of the disease, marking her on the inside because ink never did bloom on her skin?

Or what about when she showed up at my apartment, braving the sketchy part of town where I lived in an artist loft with five friends, including *boys*. How we sat on the threadbare sofa, and I jokingly offered her a shot of whiskey. The bottle was on the coffee table from the night before, when we'd toasted my first modest commission from selling a painting. She accepted the shot, and a cold chill ran through me. She came to me because she knew I could help her—that I was maybe the only person who could. I held her hand when she said, "Suzy, can you imagine, at my age?" I didn't judge when she said, "With you kids grown, I finally have a life again. No offense." Her finger circled the rim of her glass.

We planned it for when my dad was away on business. I drove her to the clinic and stayed with her for two days at home, the first day telling Dad she was napping when he called.

I didn't know then how often I would tell my dad half-truths. How it would continue long after Mom's death.

Three days before her funeral, in an uncharacteristic act of democracy, Dad tells the three of us to decide who will deliver the eulogy. We determine all of us will speak. It's only fair.

At the service, I listen to my brother and sister. To Tom's precise words, no less meaningful for their razor-sharp exactness. I smile at Diane gushing about Mom being a wonderful grandmother, how happy she is that she (she doesn't say *she alone*, but I hear it) was able to give Mom that gift.

I go last, of course, and I tone down my words, leaving only a little of the color everyone expects from me.

I don't tell that when Lucille was lost all those years ago, Mom and I sat for a long time in the drugstore parking lot, not searching. How she said maybe we should just let the *damn dog* stay lost, then maybe Dad, who took Lucy hunting on weekends, would pay more attention to her again.

I can tell my family holds their breath, just a little, until I finish. And I enjoy, just a little, my power over them.

I will not tell them that there should be a fourth of us to speak. A boy or girl who would now be twenty-two years old. A younger sibling that never was. I wonder what our brother or sister would say if they could. Would they be angry about Mom's decision, the one she questioned at times but was still glad she got to choose? Would they add to the unspoken chorus of who loved Mom more? Who loved her best? I know we all loved her best, each in our own way. But I also know there's no competition, really, because I'm the one who knew her best.

⌒

LISA FERRANTI's fiction has been a Top 25 finalist in a *Glimmer Train* contest, nominated for *The Best American Short Stories 2023*, appeared twice on the Wigleaf Top 50 Longlist, and has three times been nominated for Best Small Fictions. Her work has appeared in *RUBY, Gordon Square Review, New Flash Fiction Review, Literary Mama, Lost Balloon*, and elsewhere. She lives in Northeast Ohio with her family. Find her online at @lisaferranti or www.lisaferranti.com.

4

Could Die for Just a Wee Lie-Down

ELISSA FIELD

Beatriz had been insisting since waking that we go to the house at the top of our road, on the rise above the sea. I was barely moving—even a four-year-old should sense something amiss when the full weight of her tugging on each of my limbs has not moved the hull of me off the beached headland of the couch.

The week before Beatriz was born, a whale beached herself down on the strand, all of us from the estate barnacled, staring beneath the dune, hands covering our mouths each time the great maw gasped its epic exhale in exhaustion.

In my mind, I'm telling Beatriz this story. It is half fairy tale: titian glow of dawn gilding the silky sands of that long stretch of beach in the cup of our bay, all magic and hope. It is half cautionary tale, all the fangs and evil trees and ragged wolf pelts and failed miracles of Grimm.

Our neighbor at the top of the road, Lorna, has hung pictures of angry cats in every window of her house to discourage a chaffinch that had been concussing itself in an effort to kill his own reflection in the glass. Beatriz has seen the cats and is sure they are a sign: she had asked for a kitten. We had a cat, but he'd wandered off. Left me alone with this feral energy balled up and demanding: Beatriz tugs me by the fingers, by my elbows, my feet. "Lorna hung them for meeee… We need to goooooooo, go noowwwwwww…"

In my head, I am telling her the exact slate blue of the whale, exact slow rotation of her eye. Gorgeous death, sighing sea air—sky pink—there where our children picked shells and bits of slate, piled turrets and moats. Scientists up from the aquarium told us the whale was healthy. Not yet middle-aged. A mother. A ring of boats had garlanded the bay like some tourist postcard, doing their best to herd the whale's confused calf, not yet sure how to surface and breathe. Let alone feed. "Selfish bitch!" Lorna had hissed at my elbow. Out of habit, I'd muttered, "Sorry," without the superstition, yet, to worry that I'd hexed myself. Taken on that *sorry* and longing and broken navigation and overloaded sonar and misplaced mothering skills. I felt Beatriz somersault in the ever-tighter confines that pushed my entrails into crevices beneath my ribs, felt that giddy tickle of her hiccup, that scrape of glitter and hope. "She is still breathing," the scientist said of the whale, and Lorna had laughed at me, said I was crying when I answered, "Of course she is."

Finally, I give in—ask Beatriz, "What is it, love?" Not realizing I'm responding not to her question but her absence. My Beatriz. Her badger-dark eyes. The hedgehog-spite of her hair. Her rabbity stillness and sudden movement. The shrillness of her joy.

She has gone out, gone alone up the street to the house on the corner.

I can't breathe, of a sudden.

The weight, it must have been. Can you imagine? All your life, the utter weight of you buoyed by the crush of ocean around you. And that one time, that one time, just the once, you think, *It would be so nice to lie down.* To not swim. Not surface to breathe, not breach, not trap clouds of sardine in a blast of spiraled bubbles. Not nudge the baby, over and over, to the surface. Just. Just lie down a bit. That silken beach over yon. The way it warms with the sun. Just a lie-down, just a minute. Just a rest.

Beatriz comes back down the road to me. All those fears, but truth is, our calves don't stray, not even when they should. The bounce of light in her auburn crazed halo, the ludicrous rise of her arms like antennae, reaching for the glitter ball above a dance floor, useless for streamlining her run, useless for maintaining balance, all W*oo Woo* and celebration. Raises a picture in each hand, her miniature parade banners. My neighbor—god fuck me, if it isn't Lorna—tight-wrapping her cardigan 'round herself, smug and judgmental in Bea's wake.

"My told you, my told you!" Beatriz singsong chastises, balloon-burst of noise come back in through the door.

I'm on my "good company" behavior now—I've sat up, pushed a hand through my hair. Beatriz is in my lap in an instant, the pictures smashed against my eyes so I could see what I was too stubborn to take her to get. Lorna will move more slowly. So much judging to itemize, moving from the open back door through the kitchen. Stacked sink, open boxes, cups upon cups, heaped laundry, dropped shoes.

"It is a cat," I tell Bea, "I see that."

"Noooo," she corrects me, because again I am wrong. Pushes both pictures against my cheeks, presses hard. I might get it then. "*Two* cats!"

"You are so clever!" I praise her, because we are supposed to affirm our daughters, feed them positive images for themselves from a young age so they can see the full wide range of chances available in their future. My eyes are tracking Lorna. Sounds come from her that are not words. She is my mother tsk-ing. She is my grans.

"Ninety-one tons," I say, and my beautiful Bea asks, "Is that a lot? Is that how many cats?"

Ninety-one tons, that whale would have weighed once she'd eased herself out of water and onto land. The crush of it. Just for the sake of a lie-down. And all of them, out there in the bay, bobbing in their bright colored boats, heads turned to murmur, "Selfish bitch!" for what she'd done. For what she'd done to that little pale calf out there, cavorting in the waves.

ELISSA FIELD's fiction has appeared in *SmokeLong Quarterly*, *HAD*, *Monkeybicycle*, *Ghost Parachute*, *Reckon Review*, *The Citron Review*, *Conjunctions*, and *Adelaide Literary Magazine*. Her creative nonfiction, craft essays, and journalism have been in *Hypertext*, *Writer Unboxed*, *Sun Sentinel*, and elsewhere. She is a current emerging fellow at *SmokeLong Quarterly*, with a prior fellowship with StoryStudio Chicago. Her novels have been shortlisted for the First Pages Prize, the Heekin Foundation's award for a novel in progress, and the James Jones First Novel Fellowship. Find her @elissafield or www.elissafieldthompson.com.

5

Act As If

MIRIAM GERSHOW

In the bottom of Zadie's purse as she sits in a lightly upholstered chair at the DMV to get her license reinstated, everyone packed in side by side by side, Zadie number 23 with number 72 currently being served:

1. A half-wrapped mint filched from the bowl on the hostess stand at the Mexican restaurant Phil drove them to last

Wednesday, the mints there for the taking, but Zadie with the feeling she was stealing, Zadie always with the feeling of being caught, the unwrapped half tacky to the touch, gathering lint;

2.   Lint from wadded up tissues for nagging allergies and occasional (if no longer frequent) crying jags;

3.   One useless tampon still in its crinkly wrapper, hearkening a bygone era, testament to Zadie's wont toward accumulation, everything gathering and taking permanent root;

4.   Nicorette gum 15-pack, four pieces left, 11 hollows in the plastic packaging big enough for the tip of her ring finger to fit in and out of, like playing hidden harmonica, good for keeping her hands busy;

5.   Red chip that replaced first Zadie's beginner's-luck green chip, then later, her claw-her-way-back, mouth-full-of-hot-spit-day-after-day silver chip;

6.   Auto insurance card with a quarterly premium that could buy instead a halfway decent used couch off Craigslist, three credits at the nearest community college for training in auto maintenance or graphic design, ten bottles of single barrel straight bourbon;

7.   Flip phone she'd replaced her smartphone with, so she'd have one less thing calling out every second of every day for wanting;

8.   The signed Certificate of Completion from Tonya, the hippy (as in pear-shaped, not as in pot-smoking) teacher who lectured about response times and legal definition of impaired and classifications of drugs to a roomful of students that should have made Zadie feel camaraderie, though mostly

she was distracted by the yellow-haired girl who picked each week at the badly healing tattoo of everyone's favorite cartoon rabbit on her inner arm;

9.   Empty pack of Marlboro Reds, the insides still smelling of free fall and possibility in a way that was supposed to repel Zadie but did not;

10.   Bent-to-hell photo of her father (dead) holding Zadie and Phil's infant son (grown and gone) gazing at each other in a manner which neither gazed at her so far as she could remember;

11.   Dumb piece of paper with dumb three-word aphorism written on it that she'd referred to a startling number of times during the days and hours of her mouth full of hot spit and now just had to rub between her thumb and finger to remember its dumbness, its dumbness sometimes helping, so dumb;

12.   Key ring with her house key and her car key that she'd kept on this whole time, a carrot or a stick, she was not sure; a taunt of encouragement: *Come on, you asshole*;

13.   Empty Altoids tin, cool in her fist till she warmed it, a feeling of power in warming it. There she was. She was there. Here. Here she was;

14.   The number 23 tab she'd pulled from the dispenser after the Uber dropped her in front of the DMV, her thinking without thinking, *My lucky number*, even if Zadie had never been one to believe in such a thing—too whimsical—though 23 would be from here on out, lucky, even if she did not recognize it as such, a nameless warmth when she spotted 23 on a mile marker or in the license plate ahead of her on the back of a pickup, she misunderstanding luck as random

anointment, not of her sweat, her effort, her own hourly, daily making and remaking.

〜

MIRIAM GERSHOW's stories have appeared in *The Georgia Review*, *Gulf Coast*, and *Black Warrior Review*, among other journals. Her flash appears in anthologies from Alan Squire Publishing and Alternating Current Press, as well as in *Pithead Chapel*, *HAD*, and *Variant Lit*, where she was the inaugural winner of the Pizza Prize. Her creative nonfiction is featured in *Salon* and *CRAFT*, among other journals. She has one novel out in the world (*The Local News*), a story collection (*Survival Tips*), and a second novel (*Closer*) forthcoming.

6

Newfoundland

PHILLIP GRADY

We put our seed in the ground and buried a body, but the land gave us nothing in return for the price we paid for it, for the weight of the earth that we piled onto someone who was our own. And after such a loss, what else did we expect? We wandered through our own house. Front door impossible, backyard a stranger. Attempted to communicate with others in a language we no longer spoke. The ache inside us was no surprise, especially when it bled out into our everyday lives, venting through cracks and fractures. We pretended we had nothing left to lose, although we were wrong about that, of course. I lost you in the wet heat outside Atlanta, stuck in traffic, while you fussed with the air conditioner. We were both scorched and empty, like a kettle screaming on a burner as the water boils off into steam. You were sorry, and I was sorry, and I said goodbye so I didn't have to feel sorry all the time.

I rode trains north, carried along as if on a fast river. Seven hundred miles with a paperback thriller someone had forgotten, interrupted only by the announcements of miscellaneous towns. I abandoned the train in Washington and I hurried down the National Mall, ignoring monuments dedicated to wars and wars and murder. Things were better in Baltimore, with pit beef on a kaiser and greasy fingers, a calm looseness blooming in my head. The nights were becoming easier. I was sleeping past dawn again. In Philadelphia, I looked five years younger, and although I wasn't the person I used to be, I pretended to be that person, if only for a minute.

I was content with life in motion, suspended halfway between leaving and arriving. In Manhattan, I waded through trapped heat to Penn Station. I was excited by the idea of Providence, something that was absent from me and that I longed for. At Providence Station, I asked about beaches and how to get there, and I swam in chest-high surf. Rolling waves, one after another, the water full of stringy, rust-colored seaweed that reminded me of swimming in hair. The forest in Maine was silent in October, the floor cushioned with spent pine needles. A woman warned me about bears, and when to run, and when to puff up and yell. Sprays of steam from a teakettle on a cabin stove in thin, cold air. A reoccurring dream of Atlanta shook me from my stupor. I missed you constantly. How far away could I get from you? Where was the opposite of you? The road was the arrow of a compass pointing north.

Whenever people asked questions, I'd gesture behind me and make something up. Any other past was preferable to my own. I had a degree in history, so I was a professional. I could invent any past that I wanted. Where was I from? What work did I do?

Phoenician trader, Mesopotamian brewer, goat herding on the steppe. But not from here. From anywhere, everywhere else.

I started walking. Sometimes I dropped off the road and slept in a ditch. Days of sore feet and police with questions. I bought boots and winter clothes in Augusta. Miles of blisters. Frost on gravel shoulders. Loaves of sandwich bread smeared with peanut butter. Instant noodles cooked with hot tap water. The life of economy, with each step creating a debt inside myself that I had no means of repaying. I was spending the part of me that I couldn't hope to earn back. Poorer after every next minute, but always another mile, and a mile after that.

There was a sickness that got in me as I continued north. I began to slow down. Christmas Eve in a coffee shop, eavesdropping on two elderly men. Years spent together, their families raised as neighbors, each of them planted in the soil of their community eighty years earlier. As they talked, I was missing my own roots, which were gone. Then the old shits made racist comments about our server after she refilled the coffee cups. I fortified my coffee with cream and sugar for the extra calories, savored the hot nectar, and I was jealous. They had somewhere to go. People waiting for them.

Put a body in the ground, walk to Canada and find myself still on the same earth, as if on a treadmill, no further than where I started from.

I dreamed of you in a park with our girl, and a wind that thrashed the branches overhead and whipped your hair around. Maybe it would rain, or maybe not. "Should we go?" That's what you asked me.

I couldn't see our girl because you were in the way.

I was in a motel room in the middle of nowhere, flossing my teeth. I had a look in the mirror, and I thought: *Goddamn, aren't you a mess? You look terrible.*

But I was flossing my teeth. I was trying. The awful parts of me were trying to become better again.

Along the coast of Nova Scotia, waves pounded the beach and raked tumbling, small stones out on the recede. I was sitting cross-legged, hands tucked in my pockets, my head churning and busy.

My heart no longer hard, but heavy, living in the pit of my stomach. New Brunswick to Quebec, over the St. Lawrence and north to Newfoundland. I liked the sound of Newfoundland.

In the dead weeks before real spring, I was raw and hungry. Lips and fingertips chapped and cracked. My boots sank in mud and I worried about my feet, trying to look after them with pairs of hand-washed socks while I begged the sun overhead for warmth.

Cold mornings. Foggy, shrouding, unwelcome icy rains.

All the way to the horizon if we can, if we let ourselves, if we're doing it right, and then we turn around.

PHILLIP GRADY writes in Boston, where he is at work on a novel and a collection of interconnected short fiction. His writing has appeared in *Overheard* and *Many Nice Donkeys*.

7

The Last Laugh

M. LEA GRAY

The lingering perfume of a million flowers is so thick in the funeral home showroom that invisible rose petals plaster the inside of my mouth. Navy curtains hang heavy and block out the daylight because it really is easier to mourn in controlled lighting without the distraction of bikes and buses and joggers living, fully living the way people do under the big bright yellow sun.

A salesman in the funeral home stands over Mom and me. He's very sorry for our loss. He understands how difficult these decisions are, but does he actually understand? Has he ever watched someone die piece by piece, one day at a time, or is he like mostly everyone else who backs away because watching someone dissolve taints the memories, so friends and family, every single goddamn fucking person who said, *Whatever you need, call, I'm here for you,* is just a bag of hot air who I bet will show up at the funeral and mumble how they wish they could have done more. The salesman bows his head, so his shoulders swallow his chin, and in a short, sharp whisper, he calls the urn. Mom is holding a luxury vehicle like it's some kind of exotic ship. The urn is stainless steel. It's got that cold bluish tint, so it looks sterile. The salesman has a practiced sombre mask, and he knows exactly how long to keep a string of serious silence hanging between all three of us before he asks if we're interested in knowing *how much?*

MOM'S LAUGHTER STARTS breezy and light, fluttering through the hushed whispers rising out of the clusters of people choosing between casket and cremation. Her laughter grows out of some mutated clump of cells the size of an orange pushing against her brain. Her laughter swells from breezy into a thundering boom that levels the funeral home showroom like a shock wave, and a woman pawing through swatches of silky casket linings staggers as if some invisible hand pushed her from behind. The woman clings to a man next to her, cowering from the invisible assault. The salesman chokes on a gasp, but he recovers his solemn seriousness and tries to redirect Mom and me back to the luxury vessel's quality craftsmanship. He doesn't miss a beat as he launches into reassuring us that the remains will be *totally secure* once the urn is sealed. *The remains. The sealed remains.* Mom's laughter tapers off into a dry, hacking cough. Automatically, I pull a Kleenex out of my pocket in case her eyes start leaking, but it's not her eyes this time and by the time I get the Kleenex twisted into bullets and pushed into Mom's nostrils, three drops of blood are streaking down the potbelly of the luxury vessel. The salesman breaks his sombre mask and recoils at the sight of Mom's blood. It's probably more life than he's used to.

A fresh round of hiccupping chuckles is building, and in a minute, hysterics will have Mom doubled over, clawing for air.

THE CLUSTERS OF people in the showroom slap their hands over their mouths. So appalled. So outraged, and my god, we should know better. We should know better! They can't believe we'd steal their grief. They can't comprehend this cruel invasion into their very private, very difficult, deeply personal moment, and what kind of people are we? We have no decency. And maybe we don't have decency because that was one of the first things to go when the mutated clump of cells started pressing buttons in Mom's brain, and pee dribbles turned to soaked pants and humiliation in the supermarket checkout line while she stood in a yellow puddle, when every single son of a bitch holding their jugs of milk and bags of potatoes, who sit at tables in her diner, her fucking diner!, and know her name and ask about the family, the kids, A*ny summer vacation plans?, b*acked away from us like they'd catch whatever she had. I'll say it again, I bet they all show up at the funeral and mumble about how they wish they could have done more.

Mom flips open the urn, so her airy giggle rings through its hollow belly. She closes the lid and traps her voice like a songbird. I hope the luxury vessel seals her voice forever so I can press my ear to its stainless-steel body and listen to her laugh forever. Soon enough, Mom won't bother anybody. Soon enough, Mom will be just a collection of fading memories.

"IS THERE A better time?" The salesman avoids looking at Mom. He pleads with eyes that beg me to get Mom out of the showroom because this is a place for the dead. Can't I see that?

Mom's laughter splinters, it warbles, swells into a lump she clears out of her throat like phlegm. "What's the return policy," Mom asks.

The salesman's eyes crisscross from the question, but he tries again to regain control of the sale before the commission on this top-of-the-line urn slips out of his hands. He picks right up where he left off, and the cracks in his sombre mask smooth over, so once again, he understands how difficult this is for us, but "All sales are final."

Bloody bullets of Kleenex hang from Mom's nostrils, and no one in the showroom is even pretending not to stare. The woman from the earlier assault forgets her grief, forgets her weak state of mourning, and she rears up like a snake about to strike. The woman dares Mom to snicker just one more time, and she wags the swatches of silky casket linings like she's threatening a bratty child who could use a good wallop to put them in their place.

Mom holds the urn up to her face, huffs hot breath onto her distorted reflection, and wipes away the streaks of blood with the cuff of her sweater. "Well, I can't try it on," she says.

M. LEA GRAY is a Canadian writer who loves running trails, making soup, and watching old Roger Moore movies. She is currently hard at work on a novel-in-flash.

8

True Story

L MARI HARRIS

I watch her pocket two Snickers bars while I'm ringing up the guy who always buys a can of Skoal and a tallboy.

His name is Billy. Nice guy, friendly. Works at the tire factory or the auto shop, I can't remember which.

He's watching the girl, too, as she heads to the front doors, the afternoon sun glaring on the cases of water bottles and the rack of sunglasses.

Billy says to the girl, "Hey, I saw what you did. Put them back."

I wave Billy off and give her a look like I'm sorry we interrupted her day.

"It's okay. Go," I tell her.

Billy shoots me a look like, *What the hell? I thought you were one of the good guys.*

"She looks hungry," I offer in way of explanation.

"But stealing's not right," Billy says. "You should call the cops."

By now, the girl has slipped through the doors, and we watch her walking along the grassy median that separates the highway. Semis and $80,000 Dodge Rams whiz by, spraying her with water that hasn't drained off from last night's storms.

I can feel Billy watching me watch her. "I've seen her before. Nothing good's coming from the way she's living," he says.

"And we're doing any better?" I say, somewhere between dead serious and a joke.

Billy shrugs, slaps a twenty down, tells me to keep the change. Tells me work's been picking up lately, that it's a good time in his life and he's not messing it up again.

IN THIS VERSION, Billy shows up with some girl tagging after him.

Her hair and clothes are damp, like they'd been parked down by the river and out of nowhere she decided to jump in for a quick swim. Maybe they just met and she was trying to impress him. Maybe she slipped on a rock. Probably Billy told her, "Do this and I'll love you forever." Billy seems like that kind of guy.

Or maybe she's his wife. She looks a lot younger than Billy, but what do I know? People can surprise you. They surprise me all the time. Like that woman who comes in wearing a business suit and heels, hair in one of those fancy chignons, and buys one pack of Swisher Sweets Minis, grape flavor, that she tucks into the bottom of her purse. You'd never guess it looking at her, fancy corporate woman like that, smoking cheap cigarillos on the sly.

Billy sees me looking at the girl's wet hair and clothes. You'd think he'd offer up some kind of explanation, but he just tells her to go grab them a couple of candy bars, whatever looks good, while he points at the Skoal cans behind me.

He asks me if I've heard about the couple going around robbing convenience stores—*In broad daylight. Can you believe the balls?*—and I tell him the liquor store a few blocks over got hit last night.

"No shit?" Billy says. "Changing up their MO. That's smart."

The girl shows back up and puts two Snickers bars down on the counter.

Billy pulls a twenty out of his shirt pocket. "Yep. Keep them guessing. That's real smart." He asks the girl, "Hey, don't you think that's smart?"

"I guess," she says, not taking her eyes off the Snickers bars.

"You *guess*?" Billy looks at me like he can't believe he's having this conversation. "You *guess*? Smart and sly's where it's at. How many times I gotta go over this with you?"

THIS IS THE version I tell the cops:

He pulled a gun on *me*, not the other way around. I lunged over the counter when I saw that gun pointed in my face, grabbed his arm and we wrestled over it, because I wasn't about to die making $12 an hour where people are always shoplifting shit anyway, and besides, who am I to know what someone's going through, why they feel the need to steal candy bars or tallboys, maybe they're hungry, or maybe they had a bad day at their own shitty job.

What? Yeah, I've seen him in here before, he comes in a lot, maybe he's been casing the place; sometimes he comes in with a girl who always looks like she just rushed out of the shower, sometimes not, guy's always friendly.

Yeah, could be. Now that I think about it maybe *too* friendly. And she never talks, but today she kept yelling *Don't you hurt him!* and I'm thinking what a weird thing to say, he pulled a gun on *me*. And then I notice they both have the exact same hazel eyes, and it hits me, who the hell brings their kid along to a robbery, and then I feel this pain shoot up my arm, all the way to the shoulder, and I see his mouth moving but I can't hear him, and then my ears pop and I hear screaming, and he's looking down at the floor, up at me, down at the floor, up at me, then he's running out the doors, then you guys show up and all I can do is point toward the highway, and I can't remember the girl running after him, you'd think he wouldn't leave her behind, right? His own daughter?

No, sir, never have. Nothing good comes from having one around. Only one time I've ever held a gun. Thrust in my hand by my dad, uncle, one of Dad's friends? I can't remember anymore. Only thing I remember is how cold and heavy it was, how it wasn't at all like I'd expected, how surprised I was. It felt just like that.

L MARI HARRIS's stories have been chosen for the Wigleaf Top 50 and Best Microfiction. She lives in the Ozarks. Follow her @LMariHarris and read more of her work at www.lmariharris.wordpress.com.

9

This Time of Death

WENDY HOLMES

I was in her backyard, the tiny fenced-in yard behind an extrava-
gant Brooklyn brownstone. I had the baby, Violet, in my arms,
and my son, Jasper, was running around with Mateo—both
goofy and uncontainable. They were doing the work of four-year-
olds—transmuting the world into play. My neighbor, a petite and
fragile woman, stood silent, hands on her hips, eyes glazed over.
It was spring and the maple in her backyard stretched high above

the brownstone. The tree had been there a long time, longer than the house, perhaps longer than the neighborhood. The tree could not contain itself; little seed helicopters were spinning down on the children, the baby, my friend, and me.

"What I really need is a garden here," my neighbor said.

There clearly wasn't much light in this Brooklyn backyard for gardens. I looked up at the tree, its trunk pushing up against gravity; its branches, fractals, spreading out over her yard and into ours. All that life lifting up and soaking in the sun.

"Roses would be lovely…some Belle Amour, Floribunda, and maybe the Tuscany hybrid. I should do dahlias too…I like those Labyrinths, maybe some Shooting Stars, and definitely Arabian Nights," she trailed off.

I hadn't looked at her, kept my eye on the tree as she talked.

Then she said, "The tree will have to come down."

Six starlings swiftly flew from the branches, the boys got in a fight, and the baby started to cry.

THAT SATURDAY I heard the sound of the chainsaws wailing away at eight in the morning.

George was pissed. "What the fuck…"

I was already up with the kids, breakfast on the table and feeding Violet her oatmeal.

"What the fuck are they thinking on a Saturday morning? I'm trying to get some sleep. Jesus."

"Oh, hey…the kids…" They were both looking up at their loud and annoyed father.

I tried to calm him down. "I know, I know! I think they're cutting down that beautiful old maple."

He looked at me as if I were stupid. "I don't care about the tree. I care about my fu…my sleep." He turned on his heel and spun out of the room.

The kids and I looked at each other. Everyone's mouth open wide.

Then I heard the door slam. Still, I kept calm and continued to feed Violet, until I heard the shouting.

Standing on the sidewalk with Violet on my hip, and holding Jasper close to my other hip, I watched George cuss out Stan, my friend's husband, who was cussing back at him. Next to Stan stood his wife. Her eyes glazed over, I could only imagine she was thinking of those roses and the Arabian Nights.

The men argued, the woman stared, the tree was dying, and the children were growing as   I held them. A fierceness like a horse galloping through long grass passed through me.

"Come, Jasper, let's finish breakfast. We don't want to be a part of this."

He looked up at me and nodded.

All weekend George's loud voice rumbled and spread like a vine throughout the house as if the volume alone had the power to end all clashes, as if he were the arbiter of all that is just.

George didn't win the fight, and the tree came down that Saturday; by Sunday evening all traces of its existence in the backyard were gone.

WENDY HOLMES lives in the Hudson Valley with her puppy, Princess Aurora Borealis (also known as Squeaky). She received her MFA from the Sarah Lawrence Speculative Fiction program. She's thrilled to be included in *Fractured Lit*'s publication.

10

Diorama of Star-Crossed Lovers Driving at Night

JIM HUMES

Look at their body language: Henry grips the wheel with his left hand while the other chops at the air. Marilyn stares out the window. They are driving down a two-lane road charred silver by the summer moon.

Without saying their goodbyes, they've left a house that heaves with life. Peek inside and you'll notice sparkling teeth, crinkled faces, and hands fluttering cartoonishly. A drunk girl stirs a clutch of spaghetti into boiling water. Sodden jocks hold a séance around the sports highlights. In the backyard, clusters of teens mirror the patterns of stars above them. A boy throws up next to his car. A girl hides beside a whirring air conditioner to weep. And here—someone sits on the roof watching his cigarette smoke curl up toward the vestments of night. The scene resembles a coral reef, doesn't it? Or a just-shaken snow globe. You might ask, where are the parents? Who watches over the children?

Back to the car, their conversation, Henry's plea. He wants Marilyn to remain his true love when he leaves for college. He tells her this is the right thing, the only thing to do. Listen to the song spiriting from the tape deck—a divination of satellites and love. For her every objection, he offers the same reply: we orbit each other.

As they approach the hill that climbs out of the canyon, Henry stands on the gas. His sporty green coupe whines with all its might. On his yellow tee shirt, you might recognize *The Great Wave off Kanagawa* printed across the chest, the rowers digging into the face of that enormous, clawing wave, propelled forward by the inexorable coil of life inside them. Henry wants to fly over the crest and relieve Marilyn of the gravity that weighs her down.

She doesn't enjoy this game. As Henry's body leans forward for more speed, her fingers whiten around the grab bar next to her head. She turns her eyes forward, dark and defiant, bracing herself for weightlessness.

Now, let your attention wander up the road. A white car coming toward them bends around a curve. A woman whose face is filled with woe drinks from a Styrofoam cup. Her headlights paint the oak trees ghostly white, revealing the twine of their witches' arms. Jeweled eyes flash in the darkness—a possum, a gaze of raccoons, the green glow of a coyote sauntering along the asphalt. As the white car approaches, the woe on the woman's face disappears behind the full moon of her cup.

PEOPLE IN ACCIDENTS say they ignored the signs. The angle of the headlights drifting toward them. The mesmerizing constellation of bugs across their windshield. The slow fade of the satellite song coming to an end. Henry remembers picturing a matador dancing right and then left. He replays the details for decades:

Two tires slide off the road.

His foot remains locked down on the accelerator.

The car jerks down the embankment like a hooked fish.

A tree bends out of the way.

He steers the wheel hard right.

He reaches for Marilyn.

A mortar explodes, and everything turns upside down.

Elephant.

Feather.

Elephant.

Feather.

Coins and cassettes and papers fly like confetti.

Birds, nesting for the night, scatter.

When they come to rest, the dangling side mirror reflects a sliver of moon. The metal wadded around them ticks and tocks. Henry reaches for Marilyn, but his arm won't lift. She is curled up against her door, shutting him out yet again. Tiny roses bloom in his vision, and he begins to understand. It's been a long day. He closes his eyes, if only for a moment.

Here's a detail that's easy to miss. A few miles up the road, in a house with one glowing window, Marilyn's father, an oncologist, confronts the image of a tumor. A glass of ice water sits at his elbow. He is unaware that tomorrow, he will stand before a group of young people gathered in the ICU's waiting room and tell them that the damage to the brain stem was beyond repair ("the" brain stem, not "her," he realizes on that first anniversary as a thin keening sound splinters from his chest). The children will sit stunned by this impossibility until a girl (the one crying at the party) emits a squeak, triggering a wave of sobbing, shaking, and clutching that passes through them all. But tonight, he attributes his uneasiness to the careless ring his water glass reveals when he lifts it.

Now, back to Henry, strapped in a car that hisses its disappointment. He wears bits of glass like a crown. Blood blossoms scarlet across *The Great Wave*. Notice the flap of skin on his forehead that will leave a scar shaped like a smile. Watch his chest heave as an elephant's foot steps down and a bird flaps up against its cage. Marilyn fell in love with the long black eyelashes that flutter in his dream, the broad shoulders and impossibly strong legs curled up beneath him. She fell in love with the books that mark the trail of their tumble, the metallic tapes filled with stubbornly eclectic music that flutter in the branches.

Our job is not to project, but should you picture these two as your friends, your children, as people you once knew, you can glide into this world. Here's what I see: Henry's body heals. He dives into his studies with blinders focused only on the future. He finds another love, fair and forgiving, and they create a family complete with a son and a daughter and years of meandering happiness. But on certain nights, when the world blazes like a pearl, he feels a shadow towering over him. He takes a deep breath, ready to surrender to its weight. Then his wife's simple question, "What's on your mind?" wakens the coil of life inside him, commanding him to paddle harder, paddle faster, and fly over the history that would otherwise swallow him whole.

JIM HUMES received an MFA in fiction from San Francisco State University, where he was the winner of the Henfield Prize and the Wilner Award. He is also a recipient of the Katherine Anne Porter Prize, a Pushcart Prize special mention, and a fellowship from MacDowell. His stories have appeared in publications that include *Nimrod, Fourteen Hills*, and *Writer's Harvest*. He has been both a student and teacher at The Writers Studio and is an associate editor at *Narrative*. Originally from Texas, he lives in the redwoods just north of San Francisco.

11

Those Who Seek

LORI ISBELL

We were sitting in the stadium waiting for the Face. It came at 6:45, right-center field, or that's what I'd heard because I hadn't seen it yet.

I was there with my son and one of his friends from the city league—Kierran or Kellan, scrawny kid from the west side. Whose parents were both lawyers and bought him a three-hundred-dollar glove, which mostly he sat on so he wouldn't get dirty. Which my wife says is none of my business, but there you go.

She was at home, my wife. Said the Face was a marketing gimmick. Some digital whatever—a hologram, I think. Some way to get people to the ballpark early so they could buy more beer and nachos, nine-dollar dogs. Not even a Face, said my wife, probably a logo or something, and she wasn't driving all the way downtown in traffic when she had things to do—laundry!—by which she meant Netflix.

So, I'd brought the boys. The hot dogs weren't bad. And if seeing a game could help my son learn to lean into the plate and stop whaling at the ball like trying to bring down a plane, well, I figured, it would be worth the trip.

Because you had to make a trip if you wanted to see the Face. It didn't show up in the pictures or the videos people took, so you couldn't see it online—couldn't get it on your phone. Which pissed people off, even if it was Jesus.

That's what people were saying: the Face was the Face of Jesus. Though some said it was the Dominican reliever the team had signed, or the winner of some contest, a reality show. My buddy at work said it was the guy with the weird hair from the China thing.

I turned to my son and his friend. "Guys, you ready?"

"I'm on a level," said my son, thumbing at a tiny screen.

"For the Face," I said.

"Dad, not now."

"There he is!" said Kerwin, or Klennan, my son's friend.

But he meant the mascot—the guy in the furry suit—and the boys went back to their phones, their games. I checked my own phone: 6:43.

A nun shoved past me. The religious types were here, with the singing and praying and end of something. Or beginning. Not that I've got a problem with the religious types, of course. But if you want to hail a Mary, or amaze a little grace?—don't go putting your elbow in a man's Coors Lite.

More people mashed in, along the steps and in the aisles. Pushing into rows, trying to get a view. Most of us were on our feet and straining to right-center, when it seemed like in the distance…maybe, I thought I saw…but then the crowd heaved over and we all went down.

So I can't really say if I saw the Face or I didn't. When the bodies went horizontal—people shouting and crashing hard, on the seats, on the floor—I pulled my son and his friend close, covered their bodies with mine.

My wife wanted to know why we were home so early. I had to explain about the night and how our son cracked his screen and why we smelled like beer and mustard from the deck of Section J.

She put our son to bed.

I checked my phone for the Face.

LORI ISBELL's writing has previously appeared in *Poets & Writers*, *Inside Higher Ed*, and at the Sundance Film Festival. She is a previous winner of the Very Short Fiction Contest for the Tennessee Williams & New Orleans Literary Festival, and a semifinalist for the Eugene O'Neill National Playwrights Conference.

12

Safe Passage

ELIA KARRA

When the first of the last coughs come, I take my father to the sea. I know he likes it there. Every time memory resurfaces and reveals his previous life—before my mother, before me, long before the sting of IV lines and the smell of disinfectant—he talks about all the places he's been. The Panama Canal, the Suez Canal, the Isthmus of Corinth. Tiny, cramped spaces that are neither here nor there. All these in-betweens.

Make sure to put a coin in my mouth.
Does Charon take euros these days?
He can still walk and we walk together over sand and pebbles and green glass shards. A year ago, we were in The Hague, salt-whipped and chilled to the bone by the North Sea. Our Aegean is calmer, even this time of the year, but he's bundled up in the same coat because he can't handle the cold anymore. The shore is quiet, empty. The seagulls have come back to take their rightful place.

We used to come here when I was a kid. Every summer spent swimming and building sandcastles. My father, in the same bathing suit since his Navy days, coffee and cigarette in hand.

Did I tell you about the time we jumped in the Atlantic?
Yeah. Tell me again.
He tells me a gasping, wheezing story. He remembers some things wrong or maybe this is the first time he remembers them right. It was so cold, he tells me, they had to huddle up for hours afterward. In past retellings, he was back on duty in the engine room, sweating as the others shivered.

He shivers now, either with cold or with the echo of that day. I haven't hugged him since I was twelve and so I don't. He puts his red, steroid-swollen hands in his pockets instead and gazes at the waves, the lace of foam draped over the rocks. The skin on his face is taut, stretched thin over his skull. Smooth as the stones beneath our feet. I can't remember him any other way. When I think about childhood recitals, birthdays, those days at the beach, he looks like this: old but not old enough, too-thin torso, too-big limbs. His past selves overwritten.

I brought him here for a reason. I brought him here because his lungs are failing him and the air hurts, so maybe he doesn't need his lungs and he doesn't need the air. I take off my shoes, my socks, my jacket, lay them on the sand. My father watches, shakes his head. He always needs some coaxing.

Come. It's only water.
She cradled him once, this wine-dark sea, and she's called for him ever since. The crash of the waves, the crunch of sand. Her ghost in the conch shell he brought with him from the

Caribbean coasts. He can answer her now. There's nowhere else he has to be.

We stand ankle-deep in the water and it stings like a hundred little jellyfish. It soaks the cuffs of my jeans. The cotton sticks to my legs like a second skin. Beside me, my father begins the long, laborious trek out to the deep and I follow him, hands flying out to steady him when he falters.

And then the sea holds us, and we're weightless despite our soaked clothes, treading water as if we were always meant to. A homecoming.

But we're not built for this, not really, and transformations are slow processes. Flesh torn and reshaped, forged into something new. The sun path is short these days and by the time the first gill appears, reddened and tender on the expanse of my father's ribs, the seawater shimmers with the last of the light. He coughs, the bone-rattling cough of a dying man. He spits salt and saliva, beats the discomfort out of his chest with a fist.

Does it hurt?

No. I just have to find my sea legs.

I wait until he does. I wait until three gills form on each side of his torso, until his lungs finally rest. Until he draws water into his mouth and doesn't choke, until the last of the coughs is silenced.

Grief is to the body as silt is to water.

My stomach is full of brine when I drag myself to shore, my clothes drenched and heavy. It's dark now and I have to feel my way to my jacket, fingertips over pebbles and grit and sea glass. I gather my things and his. He's left behind a coat, a pair of shoes. A few people.

The waves crash in, reaching inland, lapping at my feet. I like to think I can still see him, in the distance, though it's dark and he's too far into the sea. In his coat pocket, I find a coin, small and shiny, round like the moon that pulls the tides. Payment for a safe passage.

ELIA KARRA is an author and filmmaker from Athens, Greece, and when they grow up, they want to be a witch. Elia has three forthcoming books: *From Athens to Reykjavik*, *Dispatches from the Otherworld*, and *Prime Time Channel Surfing*. Elia's work has appeared in *HAD*, *The Daily Drunk*, *Crow & Cross Keys*, and others. She is an associate editor for *Identity Theory* and a reader for *Twelve Winters Journal*, as well as an editor for the first *Twelve Winters Anthology*.

13

Hug Me

MIMI MANYIN

My son…he's a good boy. I hug him as often as I can. Casey is almost five now, but he's small for his age so he feels more like a three-year-old. I want to hug him like this forever. I want him to hug me back like this forever—with both arms and legs and all of his body. He won't hug me like this when he's older. I know it. He will want to hug someone else—someone prettier, someone younger, someone his age. And then I won't have anyone to hug.

I moved to the suburbs three towns over from our old house. I want to be far away from Joe so I won't run into his friends and relatives. I don't want anyone to ask about our situation. All I can rely on now is the Voila! app on my phone. Everyone loves this app. I use it to make duplicates of my favorite donut. I snap a picture with the app, press send, and voilà, a copy pops out of the Duplicator I have at home. Making duplicates feels good. I can make as many copies as I like until my stomach feels satisfied. One more chocolate-glazed donut and one more glass of wine before I go to bed. Joe is not here to remind me I'm not supposed to have any more. One is fine. The duplicates don't contain the sugar or the alcohol so it's no big deal. Slightly less palatable, but the satisfaction is real. They fill me up every time.

The bakery down the street doesn't mind people snapping pictures of their pastries inside the store as long as you buy a dozen to go. They know you can't duplicate the experience entirely. These are just copies. They look the same but don't taste the same. Not quite.

CASEY AND I used to choose together which donuts we wanted to duplicate. I always had a clean plate right by the Duplicator. I would snap a picture of the donuts and out popped the extra ones onto the plate. We had such a great time. Once in a while I also made copies of Casey's stuffed animals so he could have more friends. Casey craved hugs like me. He told me his arms would ache if he didn't have anything to hug. Seeing him surrounded by friends made me feel loved too. It made me feel like a good mother, especially when I was at work and I couldn't wrap my arms around my boy to comfort him.

I did it at my last supervised visit. Casey had fallen asleep on the couch while watching TV. Joe told me they needed to head out soon. Casey had a playdate at four so it was better for me to leave now before he woke up. Joe said all this with his back toward me as he climbed the stairs to get Casey's stuffed elephant for the car ride. He didn't even look me in the eye. Seven years of marriage! I snapped a picture of Casey as soon as Joe was out of sight. God knows when he would suddenly stop letting me come over for visits, supervised or not.

The duplication took much longer than I expected, but it worked. After putting it together limb by limb, my copy looks just like our Casey. He doesn't say or do much, but he is with me now and he is happy. When we go for walks, I dress him up warmly and let him ride in the stroller. We go shopping and we go to the park. When we get home, I let him fall asleep on my tummy and I hug him nice and tight through the night. He doesn't mind if my tears spill onto his pajamas. He knows how much I love him.

I would have made a copy of Joe too, if I'd had the chance, but he never falls asleep on the couch. He keeps his eagle eye on me at all times. He locks his fridge and his wine cabinet.

He always positions himself between Casey and me as if I'm going to do something bad.

I'm not a monster. He doesn't have to treat me like this. Mothers would never harm their children.

Joe should know that. He said I was scaring Casey. I wasn't. I just wanted to hug him. Who is going to love me now? Joe told me I needed to pull myself together. He said he still cared about me, but he couldn't be with me anymore. I told him that was bullshit. If he loved me he would have helped me instead of kicking me out. I yelled at him to prove his love and he turned his face away and wiped his eyes. He said he wished he could have the "old me" back.

I know he has a copy of me somewhere in his house because he used to love me. I don't want him to love a copy of me, though. I want him to love *me* and keep *me*.

Tomorrow, I'm going to sneak inside his house and get rid of that copy. Then I'll stay. I'll make myself huggable without all the unhealthy ingredients so both Casey and Joe will love me again.

Just one more day to go. Just one more.

MIMI MANYIN writes stories when she is not improvising on the piano. Her work has appeared in *Ploughshares, Meridian, The Greensboro Review*, and elsewhere. Mimi is a

Sewanee Writers' Conference Scholar and has also received support from the Bread Loaf Writers' Conference and Tin House Summer and Winter Workshops. She is at work on a novel and a collection of short stories. Connect with her @MimiManyin.

14

Thirteen

BETTY MARTIN

The giant orb in the night sky makes our friend's house look like a doll's house. One of us mentions this and another of us scoffs, "As if." We clutch sleeping bags in our arms, plain ones without characters. We borrow them from older siblings, or our parents buy them when they give in to our pleas. Some of us miss our Powerpuff Girls-, Sailor Moon-, or Polly Pocket-themed sleeping bags. None of us admit it. We troop inside and mutter hellos to our friend's parents who answer us with great big hellos and usher us upstairs. Our friend has turned thirteen and we are here to celebrate at her birthday party sleepover.

Everything's set up in our friend's bedroom. Candy, chips, more candy, more chips, and liter bottles of caffeinated soda; all are our appetite's desires. We dump our sleeping bags in corners. A breeze from the window tousles scraps of paper in a glass ashtray set on the floor. The scraps of paper have our noms de sorcières written on them, passed to our friends during the day at school. An orange BIC lighter our friend swiped from her parents rests nearby. We form a circle and sit cross-legged, joining hands. We evoke Hecate, Circe and Vanilla Mieux, Medea, Sabrina, and Hermione Granger. We call to Angela Leon. We call to Morgan le Fay. We ask for their blessing and then we chant our chosen names. Our friend swipes a thumb over the metal wheel on the orange BIC lighter, igniting a holy flame, setting the scraps of paper on fire. We've all seen *The Craft*.

"You better not be smoking!" shouts a parental voice from below. Our laughter floats out the window and down to the patio where our friend's parents sit smoking Newports. We watch the fire consume our names until there's nothing more to burn.

Anticlimax. Ennui. Each of us feels the letdown. No transformation presents itself. Our host saves us. "Let's do our faces!" We take out our makeup, leftover lipsticks moms have given us, Hello Kitty eyeshadow kits, and real eyeshadow kits, stolen from our older sisters. Lipstick goes on lips, eyeshadow goes on eyelids, and blusher goes on cheeks. We go creative after that, beauty marks dot green cheeks, red lipstick smears on eyelids, and eyeliner inks eyebrows as thick as caterpillars, as black as soot sprites.

We test our magical powers. One of us volunteers and lies down in the middle of the room. We each place a finger underneath and chant, "Light as a feather, stiff as a board." Our friend swears she lifts off the floor. Our power proves itself. "Now, do me!" insists another.

We grab the Ouija spirit board, daring each other to ask. "Does he like me?" Some of us replace the spoken pronoun "he" with a silent "she." "Yes," "No," "Good Bye," we hold our tender hearts in our hands until we get the answer.

"Music Time!" shrieks the birthday girl, pressing the power button on a birthday-present boom box. Two round speakers protrude from a yellow CD player. Yellow CD player eyes fill the room with sound, and we dance, careless of its gaze. Arms stretch, hands reach, torsos twist, hips gyrate. We follow the beat, the rhythm guides us. One of us grabs an empty Pringles can, an instant microphone, and lip-syncs to a sultry song. "Crank it up!" so loud we barely hear our friend's parents say, "This is positively The Last Sleepover." It makes us laugh all the harder.

Mardi Gras necklaces jangle against our chests as we jump and writhe. One of us leaps onto the bed and quirks a Britney hip thrust. Our friend's little toy poodle yaps and runs in counter-clockwise circles. Black barrettes on curly white poodle fur hop and skip and come loose. Our laughter explodes. One of us spills soda on the carpet. The little toy poodle laps it up and all of us shriek.

"I'm going up there."

"Let them have the night."

Our night. Seven best friends who are, finally, all of us, thirteen.

One last game before it's lights out, a new game we've all just heard about, not yet named, described in whispered conversations in school hallways and the girl's changing room. "Shh!" says our host, and we obey, exchanging half smiles, suppressing half giggles. Our host empties the snack bowl, and we tumble in our treasures, booty from medicine chests, bedside tables, and pocketbooks. Our friend rotates a spoon around the bowl; ovals, oblongs, and circles, white, pink, and peach, rattle together. A blindfold goes around our friend's eyes—the birthday girl goes first and closes a hand over a pill. The blindfold passes from hand to hand and we all do the same. With a show of hands, pop go the treasures into waiting mouths. A soda swig and a swallow, and now we wait.

Not for long. We dance the dance of goddesses, of sorceresses, of mages. Pores sweat, hearts pound, heads buzz, eyes divine. We're walking on sunshine. We've got the power. We have the touch, the music is in us. We commune with the cosmos and feel every particle. One of us floats to the ground. One of us falls off the bed. We lie on the floor and watch the ceiling sparkle with colors, race with contrails. One of us will haunt these kinds of parties, Skittles parties, a sweet candy name, a fun name. One of us wants to have more fun, to fly above the fog of despair thickening each day. One of us will plummet into addiction. But on this birthday night, all of us fly together over a hunter's moon, all of us dreaming, none of us knowing.

BETTY MARTIN holds a BFA from The School of the Art Institute of Chicago and an MFA from Arcadia University in Glenside, Pennsylvania, and between those degrees, she earned an MLIS from Dominican University. Her short stories have appeared in *Breakwater Review*, *Make Literary Magazine*, *Roanoke Review*, and *Cagibi*, with two stories selected for nomination for Best of the Net and the Pushcart Prize. She lives in the Midwest with her family and a rescue cat named Max.

15

The Children

SARA MCKINNEY

When the Children came back, they came back different. Dante had an arm that wasn't his attached at the shoulder. You could tell because of how long it was, much longer than the other, and the fact that it was on backward. Rachel, who always talked so much before, couldn't talk at all except to let out a little screaming laugh when you bumped into her, and Maggie, well, some sort of animal must have got at her because her face had chunks missing.

We didn't quite know what to do with them, although of course the parents were happy. New toys were purchased, old bedroom furniture repainted in bright, smiling colors. They brought the Children's clothes out of storage and washed them, so the Children didn't have to keep wearing the suits and dresses (now quite musty and moldy in places) that they were buried in.

In school the Children sat silently, stiffly, facing forward at their desks, unblinking. This was true even of Jimmy who used to be such a clown, throwing pencils at the ceiling and performing acrobatic dismounts from the top of his desk, but now he never laughed or spoke except to say please and thank you in a voice that creaked like a door hinge left unoiled for a century. Their homeroom teacher confided in me one afternoon when we ran into each other in the hallway that she was leaving them alone more and more often, sneaking into the lounge or the bathroom to sip from a small glass bottle while the Children stared obediently at the chalkboard. When she came back they were always exactly where she left them.

"It's the stillness," she said, her hand on my arm as if it were a banister on a staircase she couldn't quite trust. "The perfect stillness, I can't stand it. There's something still dead about them. They're alive but not really. They don't breathe, I've noticed."

I frowned at this; the teacher was a downer and always had been. Everybody knew it. I rather liked the Children in their new state, even the ones who hadn't come out totally intact, but instead leaked juices onto the carpet or belched out centipedes and beetles. There was something lovely about their wanness, coldness, stiffness, how you could look out on the schoolyard and see them playing the way they played now, no running or jumping or screaming, only sitting in neat pewed rows while one of them lay on the ground, eyes closed as if sleeping and at peace. Their positioning was always expressive, finely articulated in the tilt of heads and necks, the way a doll's might be. Death had fashioned them all into actors.

It was nice to think sometimes that in a kinder world my own son might have been among them, his own wanness, coldness, stiffness endearing him to the other Children. I imagined them passing the small swaddle of his body back and forth, incorporating it into their scenes of mourning, a younger sibling, a prop and a wonder. I imagined wiping the soil from his skin and teaching him to play like them, quietly laying him to rest, not in another coffin, but in the crib that stood, unused, in my attic. Now play dead, I would say, and he would die, temporarily and incompletely, his bright green eyes watching me from under the lids. But my son was not like the other Children; my son had been born dead. There was no life to return to his body, and so he stayed below.

"Well, it's not their fault," I sniffed. "We asked them to come back. And they're a bit too young for labels." This was true, although none of them would ever grow any older. Before she could respond, I headed back to the lounge, because I didn't want to hear it. What right did she have to complain about them, anyway? Certainly, our jobs had become easier. The Children were, if nothing else, well-behaved, as sweet as any mother's dream.

SARA MCKINNEY is the managing editor of *The Milton Review* and holds an MFA from the University of Arizona. Her writing appears in or is forthcoming from *BOOTH*, *Jewish Fiction*, *Rubbertop Review*, and elsewhere. Learn more at www.saramckinney.com.

16

When the Giant Breathed

ZACH MOSER

In 2023, the island known in County Kerry as the Sleeping Giant, named for its resemblance to a man lying on his back, exhaled. Those first few people to see it were quick to dismiss the notion they must have seen mist rising or a flock of gulls. For, as they explained, they had seen the chest of the Giant sink, then rise. In only a few hours, the people of the Dingle Peninsula on the west coast of Ireland, just east of the island, had nearly all seen for themselves that the Sleeping Giant had indeed exhaled. And continued to do so throughout the day and into the evening.

When a length of brownstone that could only be an arm slowly inched into view on the westerly side of the island, even the oldest Dingle men in their drinks, whose brows were furrowed in a never-ending scowl of suspicion, suddenly raised the tips of their caps, eyes widening in deep alarm. The Sleeping Giant was breathing and it was no longer sleeping.

Schoolchildren were rushed home, restaurants closed their doors and turned off their gas, the pubs stayed open, and the fire towers set up 24-hour watches with binoculars and floodlights aimed at the Sleeping Giant who inch by inch over the course of a week lifted a great earthen hand up above the curve of its belly. In the towns on the small peninsula, villagers rushed from house to house to trade news and misgivings. As they ran across thin cobblestone streets, their heads were tugged toward the island as if beckoned by the slowly rising rock.

When another brown tract of land rose from the sea on the easterly side of the island, and five hard fingers breached the turquoise surface of the sea, the wind picked up. The weather could change from one street to the next on a normal day in Dingle, but three weeks after the Sleeping Giant first exhaled, a cold wind began to pound steadily from the direction of the island.

Every day the Giant rose farther out of the Atlantic, and every day the gale winds blew fiercer. Shutters clapped and handkerchiefs were ripped out of people's pockets. Sheep, oblivious to the growing shadow in their farmers' lives, were blown like white tumbleweeds across the pastures. One shrewd farmer tied bricks of peat to his herds' hind legs. This worked for only a few hours before the animals decided their weights were tastier than the grass and ate away each other's anchors. The farmer came out later that night to see his sheep pinned against his far gate, baa-ing indignantly.

After four weeks, the Sleeping Giant was sitting up, its head bowed to its chest as if still drowsy. Some on the peninsula fleetingly thought to call the taoiseach in Dublin but decided that as the problem was off their shores, it was theirs alone to endure.

The Iveragh Peninsula to the south thought the same. When a constable from a seaside town peered north one night and saw the Sleeping Giant bent over, twice as high as normal, he said to his wife, "They'll be having trouble up around Dingle, I imagine." The Irish government would not have been much help anyway. Irish Rugby was preparing for the quarterfinals of the World Cup, their eighth visit, and most folks had their focus invested on the pitch.

The villagers' disquiet turned to dread when on the fifth week, the Sleeping Giant's head turned toward them. Neighbors stopped visiting each other's homes, the only gesture of community was blinking flashlights from slatted windows. Even the pubs were silent, drinks ordered with finger raises rather than words. There were no songs. The wind was too loud. And every night, the young children cowered together under the sound of gnashing and grinding as the Giant rose ever upward.

When the Sleeping Giant rose to its feet, bent in a squat, rain, hail, and wind smashed into the peninsula with hurricane force. Families moved beds into basements, preparing for when the Sleeping Giant finally stood. Generations of Dingle families looked out over the ocean to see their friendly island. Now, to find out it had been a monster in the mist, many were surprised to find strands of betrayal mingling with the nest of fear and worry cocooned in their chests.

Six weeks after the Sleeping Giant first exhaled, at midnight, the wind died. Families in their basements awoke, shocked by the sudden silence. Men and women in the pubs put their drinks down and looked over bent shoulders as moonlight peeked through the boarded-up windows and painted their faces. And then a mighty roar.

Cracking stones erupted, winds screamed over the island like banshees, and rain drummed angry as a military tattoo. Every light on the peninsula was extinguished and fathers and mothers held their children, and those in the pubs held their drinks and occasionally each other.

The next morning, to everyone's shock, the sun rose. One brave child sprung from his bed and raced outside. His mother screamed after him but when she went out, she fell silent. Just as everyone did that morning. Fences were twisted into balls, windows were shattered, and fish lay all over the streets, some still flopping. But the damage was not total; only one man died. The farmer who had tied peat to his flock had tried the same trick with cement blocks only to receive a kick from a fed-up ewe right to his temple.

Out on the ocean, the Sleeping Giant was gone. The people smiled at each other, but only because they were supposed to, they had survived the danger after all. But in their hearts, something ached. There was a hole in their ocean where an island once stood. They cupped their eyes, searching for the monster who had made its home along the same blue-and-green coast that they themselves had loved so well.

〜

ZACH MOSER is a freelance writer from Philadelphia, Pennsylvania. He writes in a variety of genres and has published works in *McSweeney's Internet Tendency*, *The NoSleep Podcast*, and *Screen Rant*. You can see what he's been working on at www.thezachmoser.carrd.co.

17

Self-Preservation

DANIELLE MUND

In the first month of the year after the holiday season she felt out of sorts (the season she got the diagnosis, the season the doctor gave her a referral to the Giant Hospital), Barbara bought things. She awoke every day with the phrase *carpe diem* on a looping conveyor belt in her mind, showered in frigid water as soon as it shot from the showerhead (to wait for it to turn hot was the difference between life and death), and dressed quickly and simply, for it was imperative she be at the Big Lots! when the doors opened at nine. Not getting coffee at Starbucks across the street, not parking in the parking lot, but actually standing at the door. If she wasn't, she'd already lost out on the possibility of claiming the entirety of the day's clearance rack, lost the day's meaning. Once she was inside and had chosen the right shopping cart she wheeled it directly to the farthest point in the store and began scavenging down the aisles. She loaded up on whatever was on sale, toothbrushes and bath bombs, Connect4 and Barbie dolls, bras too big and too small, leftover tinsel, a dog bed, a Discman with AM/FM radio, a swiveling office chair. She gathered them as a squirrel gathers acorns, each day collecting and organizing and storing, and just as a squirrel buries its treasure in the space between the heavens and the inferno, so Barbara rocked herself into a trancelike state between the aisles of her own meticulous making at home: *Apparel, Holiday Decor, Office Supplies.* Day after day she returned to the ever-changing display at the front of the store where a carousel of discounted items from electronics to baby bibs required a Tetris-like rearrangement of items in her cart. On the morning she cracked the puzzle without once having to take an item out before putting it back in again, she let out an audible "Amen," and that afternoon arranged things at home without rocking. By then she was placing things not in the house but behind the garage, where there was a broken refrigerator she'd found by the side of the road. The fridge had compartments, and that was its point. Because she had a nagging feeling that lining things up along the backside of the garage could be considered the beginning stage of something unspeakable (she did not know what it was exactly, but it had to do with avalanches of tools, hidden insect nests, getting lost without anyone ever realizing), she told herself she was placing things outside only until her husband *cleaned up his stuff,* only until the exterminator came, just until she could find the stove, only putting things in a new place because it was more spacious, easier to see, only because things had a way of getting away from her in the house just when she needed them. The fridge reminded her that compartmentalizing was key, that preservation was crucial.

Outside she didn't have to worry about an avalanche when she rocked, outside she could stack things farther apart so they could breathe. Space was essential for creating new walls. Sometimes Big Lots! ran out of clearance items, and she'd have to go to Walmart or Target or search for some immaculate yard sale in another ramshackle town along the Hudson, pick up clues leading to the dump at the far end of town, find decaying toilet bowls or fish tanks. When that happened she moved cautiously, limited only by her truck's size, feeling, finally, the importance and care each item required of her, the mendable lawn mower, the patchable coveralls, the fractured mirror, the ripped duvet, the oozing boom boxes, the jigsaw that occupied her whole mind, body, and soul.

So that she never needed help she kept a jack (or three, and a detachable folding hauling bed, ready whenever she needed it) in the back of the truck. She could lift a whole rusted-out car with two hands (slip the jack under its belly, forget the wheels, wheels fall off, wheels were to be organized separately anyway) and she hauled in dishwashers, boilers, dryers. Sometimes she would stand on top of the largest mound and stare out at the overwhelming security around her (she always tried to make eye contact with the landfill manager, a sign of impregnable mental control, nothing ever lost in her world) and then she would shuffle back between the heaps, letting the natural bulwarks guide her to the sagging truck. In the first month of the year after the holiday season she felt out of sorts, the season she got the diagnosis, the season the doctor gave her a referral to the Giant Hospital, a horrible season to exist, Barbara welcomed 4,798 treasures big and small onto her property. Sometimes in the late afternoons the terror would course through her bloodstream, form a new growth in her brain, shoot her in the eye with vivid visions of rectangular wooden boxes and yellow carnations and insect-filled dirt and the inevitability of what she'd already created for herself in this world, but all that disappeared when she was amongst her things.

DANIELLE MUND is a proud native of New York City, currently based in Puerto Rico where she lives with her husband and two young daughters. When not bemoaning the year-round warmth and beachy lifestyle, she can be found in a dark corner getting lost in her art or words, likely sipping on a hot cappuccino. Most recently, she was shortlisted in the New Writers Flash Fiction Competition and published in the Bath Flash Fiction Award's 2023 Anthology.

18

We Went to the Museum

CHRIS NEGRON

We went to the museum, but we didn't see anything good.

We sat on a long bench under the great T-Rex, frozen in midroar. Outside, your son wound his way through a fake rainforest, raised pathways running under and over each other. He had darted for the doors as soon as the tickets were paid for. Escaping.

"Go with him," you told your husband.

The sun spiked its rays between the branches, every few minutes shining straight into our eyes. Every few minutes making us squint. Every few minutes causing us to raise our hands to block out the unwanted light as we lost sight of our families. My wife. Your husband. Your son.

"I can't see him anymore," you said.

We were surrounded by the past, but focused only on the future.

The adults laughed as your boy led them around in mad circles. They doubled over, out of breath. Even they, the healthy ones, couldn't keep up with him. Or maybe they weren't trying hard enough. Maybe they were letting him run, because, lately, it was all he seemed to want to do.

"They'll be all right," you said.

And I couldn't tell if it was a question or not.

We came here to talk, but that turned out to be harder than expected.

The silence was much easier. It came naturally, carried aloft by the pain that enveloped us both, transmitted by senses dulled by pills and injections. I shrugged my shoulders and gripped my cane harder whenever I felt myself slipping. You shifted and twisted your hips every time your colostomy bag pinched your skin wrong.

Eventually, words came. Some anyway. College, stepmother, IRAs. Next husband, graduation, wedding. First girlfriend, prom. Remember to laugh, take care of my plants, don't give away my comics.

Your son returned triumphant, pressing his breathless grin into the glass. Our spouses walking twenty feet behind him, talking with heads down, hands tucked deep into pockets, wrists clutched behind backs. They caught us watching and forced smiles onto their faces, sent too-enthusiastic waves our way.

We were the ones dying, but they were the ones it was killing.

"I'm going to miss it," you said.

Slipping, slipping, slipping. I shrugged my shoulders. Gripped my cane harder. Straightened my posture.

The movie was about to start. Something about whales. In the museum we went to, different movies played every hour, but this particular one, only once per day. Your son loved whales, so we waved them all toward the theater.

"Try not to miss any of it," you said.

"It only happens once," you said.

They begged for us to join them, but we were too tired. Still, your son lingered. He leaned against your legs and glanced above you, straight at the giant teeth of the T-Rex. His curious eyes followed the old dinosaur's bones from head to tail and back again.

He tore his gaze away from the old fossil and his hands shot straight into the air. He winked his fingers open and shut. Obediently, your husband took one, my wife the other. They pulled him free from you.

And you did not reach out. And you did not try to force him to stay.

One last time, they—your husband, my wife—asked us to join them. They pointed up at the theater, not more than thirty feet away.

There's even an elevator, they said.

We answered no. One last time.

Shoulders slumped, the two of them trudged up the ramp toward the double-doored entrance. Your son skipped faster and bobbed higher between them with each step closer. Closer to the whales and the ocean, to the deep blue, to the waiting nothingness.

Closer, closer, closer. Closer and farther at the same time.

Because we followed them, but only with our eyes.

CHRIS NEGRON is the author of several novels for children, among them Georgia Author of the Year finalist and Sakura Medal nominee *Dan Unmasked* and his latest, *Underdog City*. He holds a computer science degree from Yale University, but his writing is fueled by his many other interests, including comic books, sports, and competitive cooking shows. Visit him at www.chrisnegron.com.

19

Flesh Wounds

TANYA NIKIFOROVA

"He's bleeding out!" These words stampede through the air, dis-embodied from their owner. "Somebody help him!"

I stand on the museum steps. When the words reach me, I am unsteadied by their desperate velocity, and I wobble on the bottom step.

I hope they have reached ears besides my own, but the green lawn abutting the museum, usually speckled with undergrads, is empty. For reasons I can't understand and will dissect later, I move toward the voice.

Around the corner of the museum entrance, I find a woman with her back to me, kneeling on the grass as she holds a phone in trembling hands and dials 911.

She sees me, and gasps.

"He's bleeding out," she says, softly now. "Help him."

In front of her, a man lies on a red blanket. His eyes are closed and his lips are slightly parted. I gawk, stupidly, letting seconds pass. Professor Liang's words are in my head: Don't just look, Kate, *see.*

No, it's not a blanket he's lying on.

He is lying in a pool of blood.

I note hues of cadmium, carmine, and amaranth. And the smell of earthy rot.

Across his neck there are two short slits that just barely break the skin. But on the left side of his neck, where one usually goes to feel their pulse, there is a third puncture, this one cavernous and deep, and blood gurgles like a brook through this opening.

"*Help him,*" the woman whispers hoarsely.

I pat down my body, confirming that I have nothing to apply pressure with. I look at my hands. They handle cancerous turpentine, resins, and pigments all day, but the idea of using them to touch a stranger's blood feels perilous.

I see two young women gathered, maybe ten feet away. "Can you give me a piece of clothing?" I ask. The one on the left looks disgusted, like I'm asking her to strip naked. The one on the right removes a flannel shirt tied around her waist and throws it to me.

I crumple it up and press it to the man's neck. I hold pressure with the shirt, and blood starts to soak through. I press harder. When I look up to say thank you, they are gone.

"They're asking if he has a pulse," the woman calling 911 says.

Not being able to check his neck as I am practically choking him with the shirt, I feel along his left arm. I can't find it at first by the wrist, but then there it is. A weak, thready thump beneath my thumb.

"Yes, I think so," I yell back.

For the first time, I look at the man's face. He is in his sixties or seventies, with a thin smear of gray, matted hair. He is cleanly shaven. He wears a short-sleeve khaki button-down shirt that is tucked into suit pants with freshly pressed creases. A sunken stomach bows beneath a fine leather belt. In the palm of his open hand lies a small kitchen knife, the kind you use to peel an apple, with an ochre wooden handle. While holding pressure with my right hand, I use my left hand to move the knife away and stick its sharp side down into the dirt.

"They said keep holding pressure," the woman yells. "They're on their way." And then, "Hurry, please," she pleads into the phone, and reminds them, "There's a lot of blood here." The man opens his eyes. "You're hurting my neck," he says, but doesn't move to stop me.

He doesn't reach for the knife. "Let me die," he says.

"I can't, I'm so sorry," I tell him.

What am I sorry for? The pain I'm causing him? Or for keeping him alive?

And then he slips into unconsciousness again.

On the orders of my professor, I was here to walk through the Gauguin exhibit for inspiration. On her last feedback form, Professor Liang wrote, "Technically proficient. Completely uninspired." Last week in class she temperamentally paced as we painted. When she stood behind me, she asked, "What are you trying to say here?" I just wanted to paint things perfectly and beautifully, but so far in my MFA, I have learned only that beauty is the opposite of art. "Nothing," I told her, defiant. "I thought so," she said, and walked away.

I resolve to paint him the way I found him.

Yet I fear that the stress of this moment will overwhelm me afterward. I will disremember every detail when I sit down to sketch, and without the details, I will fail.

I take the knife out of the ground and place it back in his hand. Still holding pressure on his neck, I take my phone out of my back pocket. I bring it to my face to unlock it.

The woman who called 911 is leaning against a tree, looking at the ground and rocking gently. By the low wail of the sirens, I can tell they are a few blocks away.

I remove the shirt from his neck carefully. The main wound is no longer bleeding. I bring my phone close to his neck. When I take the first picture, the camera app makes that automatic clicking sound.

The woman looks up, horrified. "What are you doing?" she asks. I don't say anything. Instead I take a few steps back and take a photo of his face, and then of his body. I am now standing over him, capturing every angle.

"This is disgusting, YOU are disgusting," she hisses at me.

"You wouldn't even touch him. You waited for me to get here, just letting him bleed out," I say calmly.

And then I hear her make a little "Ohhh" sound as she looks down.

He is bleeding again, and now, instead of a slow gurgle, the blood pulses out of his neck rhythmically. I keep snapping.

The sirens grow louder. There isn't much time left.

Any second now, help will arrive.

TANYA NIKIFOROVA is a primary care physician who writes fiction and poetry inspired by the breathtaking range of human experiences she encounters in her profession. A first-generation immigrant from Belarus, she resides in Pennsylvania with her husband and daughters, where she also tends to a garden and runs.

20

The Life of the Mother

SUSAN PERABO

Following the meeting with the doctor, there was no thought of a baby shower. Too much rage. Too much grief. The two were indistinguishable, separate ropes twisted into a single noose. Bullshit about *stages of grief*, the mother thought; it was everything all at once. Including this: she was nonstop clammy from morning sickness. Before the diagnosis, she sometimes dry heaved predawn in the downstairs half bath, so as not to wake anyone. After the diagnosis, she didn't care; she just bowed over the side of the bed and dry heaved into the wicker wastebasket. After the second time the father lined the wastebasket with a garden-scented bag.

They sought a second opinion, then a third. "It's extremely rare," the third doctor had said of the mother's condition. Seated behind an antique desk, the doctor removed her glasses. "This…" she began. "This is…kind of our nightmare scenario."

"There has to be something we can do," the father said. Oh, he had some ideas. Once, in a movie he loved, a vicious man had punched his wife in the stomach, and that had been the end of that. Could he punch his wife in the stomach? The father tried to picture it, couldn't even get past the act of making a fist.

In the fourth month the morning sickness subsided, but the mother was weak, dazed. Her stools were laced with blood. She couldn't sit without pain, so spent much of the day in bed, or stretched out on her side on the living room couch. She tried to spoon her daughter, but Allie wasn't having it, slithering out from under her arm as soon as the mother's embrace loosened even a fraction.

Her parents rented an Airbnb a half mile away. When she asked how long they'd reserved it for, they wouldn't say. They stayed at the house during the day while the father was at work. The grandfather flipped through the cable channels but kept the TV on mute. The grandmother played Candy Land with Allie while the mother watched from the couch across the room.

In the fifth month, she woke one morning, rolled over with effort, and said to the father, "Let's do it."

"Do what?" he asked. He'd been awake for hours. Most nights he only slept from 3 to 5 a.m., when his body shut down and buried him in a dreamless, thick ink. In the moments before the ink all he could think of was how he would possibly survive afterward, a single father with a three-year-old and a baby, or a three-year-old and a disabled baby, or a three-year-old and a dead baby.

"Let's have a shower," she said.

For a moment he thought she was suggesting they have sex, and he felt such a shocking juxtaposition of desire and terror that he only gaped at her.

"We should get everyone together," she said. "It would be good for my mom. My sisters. And Allie."

"What about you?"

She scoffed. "What about me?" she asked.

THE FATHER AND the grandmother had been at odds for weeks, which they both recognized had nothing to do with either of them, yet they kept finding things to argue about. Now, in the kitchen, they argued about the shower. About flowers—the father wanted them, the grandmother did not. About presents—the grandmother wanted them, the father did not.

"What kind of presents are people supposed to bring?" he asked. "Seriously."

"She wants it to be normal."

"Then why not have flowers?"

"Flowers are for funerals," the grandmother said flatly.

None of this mattered, because just then the mother shuffled into the kitchen and announced that not only were there going to be flowers and presents, goddammit, but there would also be blue and white streamers and *It's a Boy* balloons, frilly napkins, champagne punch, and vanilla cupcakes decorated with cute teddy bears.

"Sweetheart," the grandmother said.

"I want it to be NORMAL," the mother shouted. (The mother never shouted. She didn't even recognize her own voice.) "You can't pick and choose. It's all or nothing. It's normal or it's not. And it's going to be normal."

There was nothing they could say. At this point, they'd be cruel to try to talk her out of anything. Instead they looked past her and at each other with seething resentment. They both so desperately wanted someone to blame.

ALLIE AND THE girl cousins wore matching purple dresses. Purple was the mother's favorite color. She had invited almost everyone she knew: old roommates, former colleagues, neighbors she rarely spoke to. No one wanted to go, but how could anyone refuse? The champagne punch was gone in an hour. The aunts stood in the kitchen with a bottle of peach schnapps on the counter between them. Last month one of the aunts had found a doctor in Canada. There'd been whispered plans. Then the doctor and four of his patients were arrested and charged with murder.

The mother opened presents. The grandmother sat beside her, making a list in loopy cursive of who'd given what, knowing she would be the one sending thank-you notes. Jamie: Hippopotamus blankets; Gretchen: Truck onesies; Ashley K.: Spiderman rattle.

A friend from college wept openly until the father finally escorted her to her car.

Someone threw up at the base of the black walnut in the backyard.

The body inside the mother was busy growing in all the wrong places. If he lived, the baby boy would be swaddled in the hippopotamus blankets. He would wear the truck onesie. One day, he would reach out and grasp the Spiderman rattle. If he lived, all the people in this room would tell him stories about his mother. They would say, she chose you. And he would believe it until he was old enough to know better. He would believe it until one day he was old enough to understand that the only thing his mother had chosen were the cupcakes.

⌒

SUSAN PERABO is the author of the collections of short stories *Who I Was Supposed to Be* and *Why They Run the Way They Do*, and the novels *The Broken Places* and *The Fall of Lisa Bellow*. Her fiction has been anthologized in *The Best American Short Stories*, *Pushcart Prize*, and *New Stories from the South*, and has appeared in numerous magazines, including *One Story*, *Glimmer Train*, *The Iowa Review*,

The Missouri Review, and *The Sun*. She is Writer in Residence and Professor of English at Dickinson College in Carlisle, Pennsylvania, and on the faculty of the low-residency MFA program at Queens University. She holds an MFA from the University of Arkansas, Fayetteville.

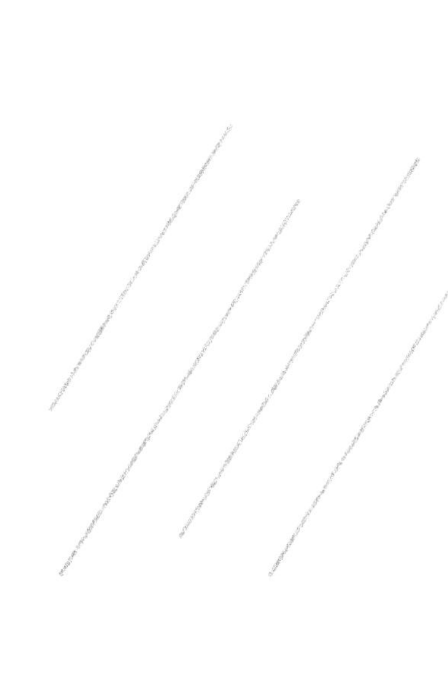

www.ingramcontent.com/pod-product-compliance
Lightning Source LLC
Chambersburg PA
CBHW060507300726

48975CB00008B/2687